Dear Parent:

Congratulations! Your child is taking the first steps on an exciting journey. The destination? Independent reading!

STEP INTO READING® will help your child get there. The program offers books at five levels that accompany children from their first attempts at reading to reading success. Each step includes fun stories, fiction and nonfiction, and colorful art. There are also Step into Reading Sticker Books, Step into Reading Math Readers, and Step into Reading Phonics Readers—a complete literacy program with something to interest every child.

Learning to Read, Step by Step!

Ready to Read   Preschool–Kindergarten
• big type and easy words • rhyme and rhythm • picture clues
For children who know the alphabet and are eager to begin reading.

Reading with Help   Preschool–Grade 1
• basic vocabulary • short sentences • simple stories
For children who recognize familiar words and sound out new words with help.

Reading on Your Own   Grades 1–3
• engaging characters • easy-to-follow plots • popular topics
For children who are ready to read on their own.

Reading Paragraphs   Grades 2–3
• challenging vocabulary • short paragraphs • exciting stories
For newly independent readers who read simple sentences with confidence.

Ready for Chapters   Grades 2–4
• chapters • longer paragraphs • full-color art
For children who want to take the plunge into chapter books but still like colorful pictures.

STEP INTO READING® is designed to give every child a successful reading experience. The grade levels are only guides. Children can progress through the steps at their own speed, developing confidence in their reading, no matter what their grade.

Remember, a lifetime love of reading starts with a single step!

For Amy, who has always loved
Beautiful Pink Hairbows
—M.D.A.

For Holly and Connor
—K.S.B.

Text copyright © 2002 by Marsha Diane Arnold.
Illustrations copyright © 2002 by Karen Stormer Brooks.
All rights reserved under International and Pan-American Copyright Conventions. Published in the United States by Random House Children's Books, a division of Random House, Inc., New York, and simultaneously in Canada by Random House of Canada Limited, Toronto. Originally published by Golden Books, an imprint of Random House Children's Books, a division of Random House, Inc., in 2002.

www.stepintoreading.com

Educators and librarians, for a variety of teaching tools, visit us at
www.randomhouse.com/teachers

Library of Congress Cataloging-in-Publication Data
Arnold, Marsha Diane.
Edward G. and the beautiful pink hairbow / by Marsha Diane Arnold ; illustrated by Karen Stormer Brooks.
    p.   cm. — (Step into reading. A step 3 book.)
SUMMARY: When her neighborhood friends come over for their weekly meeting to trade things, Evelyn finds that Cynthia Lucinda will trade her pink hairbow for Evelyn's cute but demanding baby brother.
ISBN 0-307-26337-1 (trade) — ISBN 0-307-46337-0 (lib. bdg.)
[1. Brothers and sisters—Fiction. 2. Barter—Fiction. 3. Clubs—Fiction.]
I. Brooks, Karen Stormer, ill.   II. Title.   III. Series: Step into reading. Step 3 book.
PZ7.A7363 Ed 2003   [E]—dc21   2002013411

Printed in the United States of America   11 10 9 8 7 6 5 4
First Random House Edition

STEP INTO READING, RANDOM HOUSE, and the Random House colophon are registered trademarks of Random House, Inc.

Edward G.
and the Beautiful
Pink Hairbow

by Marsha Diane Arnold

illustrated by Karen Stormer Brooks

Random House 🏠 New York

This is my little brother, Edward G.

He doesn't talk much yet,

but he sure knows how to insist.

At breakfast, he insists on

smashing bananas in my hair.

When I'm practicing piano,
he insists on banging
Mom's pots and pans.

5

And every night
while Mom fixes dinner,
he insists I read his
favorite story a thousand times.

If Edward G. didn't insist so much,
there wouldn't have been a problem
last Wednesday afternoon.

On Wednesday afternoons,
all the kids in the neighborhood
meet in my room for our weekly
Trade-Ya Club.
It's a good way to get
something you've always wanted,
like Anna's glittery bangle bracelets.

And it's a great way to get

rid of things you *don't* want,

like that orange and green sweater

Aunt Julie knitted for me.

Last Wednesday,

I taped a sign on my bedroom door.

"Edward G.," I said, "pay attention.

This sign says,

NO LITTLE BROTHERS ALLOWED.

That means you."

Edward G. made a funny face.

He headed toward the kitchen,

banging Mom's best pot with a spoon.

I rolled my eyes.

Then I closed the door

and waited for the Trade-Ya Club.

Anna arrived first.

"Look, Evelyn J.," she said.

"I have a whole wagonload
of comic books to trade."

Marcus brought his action figures.

Jamie carried a box full of
plastic dinosaurs.

Carlos had a bag filled with marbles—
moonstones and cat's-eyes.

Shoko skated in on
a yellow skateboard.
She carried a
red skateboard
in her arms.

13

Cynthia Lucinda arrived last.
She twirled around the room,
showing off as usual.

"Today," said Cynthia Lucinda,
"I've brought my grandmother's
one-of-a-kind hairbow to trade.
I'll bet none of you has anything
worth trading for it."

"Looks like a regular
old hairbow to me," said Carlos.
But Carlos was wrong.
Cynthia Lucinda was wearing
the most Beautiful Pink Hairbow
in the world.
She knew it was beautiful.
And she wanted a lot for it.

Right away, I started looking

through my closet for some

fancy dress-up clothes to trade.

I knew Cynthia Lucinda

loved fancy dress-up clothes.

That was when Edward G.

peeked his head into my room.

"No little brothers allowed!" I yelled.

I pointed to my sign.

Edward G. had smashed bananas on it.

"He can't read your silly sign,"

said Cynthia Lucinda.

"He's only a baby."

18

19

I closed my bedroom door tight.

Edward G. banged on it.

"Oh, let him in, Evelyn J.

He's so cute,"

said Cynthia Lucinda, opening the door.

"But he doesn't have

anything to trade," I said.

"Except pots and pans," laughed Jamie.

I was upset.

First, Edward G. was in my room and wouldn't leave.

Second, I didn't have anything good enough to trade for Cynthia Lucinda's Beautiful Pink Hairbow.

But I wasn't giving up.

"Cynthia Lucinda,

isn't this the neatest hat

you've ever seen?" I said.

Cynthia Lucinda ignored me.

She was too busy

admiring Edward G.

"Cynthia Lucinda."

I tried again.

"This purple dress is
perfect with the hat."
But Cynthia Lucinda was
still ignoring me.

Now she was tickling
Edward G.
Just as she leaned over
to give Edward G. a big hug,
somebody yelled, "Trade ya!"

Dinosaurs and marbles
and comic books started flying.
Carlos traded three cat's-eyes
and a moonstone for Anna's
"Manfred the Magnificent"
comic book.

Jamie and Marcus traded
five action figures and
one Tyrannosaurus Rex
for Shoko's red skateboard.

And I traded Edward G.
for the Beautiful Pink Hairbow.

After Cynthia Lucinda took
Edward G. home, things were
nice and quiet in my house.
I didn't have to worry about
smashed bananas in my hair.
So, I clipped my Hairbow
right on top of my head.

I didn't have to wear

earmuffs to practice piano.

Instead, I wore my

Beautiful Pink Hairbow.

And I didn't have to read
Edward G. his favorite story
a thousand times while Mom
fixed Wednesday night meat loaf.
With my extra time, I tried on
all my dress-up clothes to see which
went best with the pink in my Hairbow.

At dinner, Mom got a little upset
when Edward G. didn't show up.
I had to explain all about my
Beautiful Pink Hairbow.
"Evelyn J.," she said quietly,
stabbing her meat loaf a few times,
"bring Edward G. home right now."

I filled my wagon with my
three favorite sticker books,
my teddy bear backpack,
five stuffed animals,
and lots of dress-up clothes.
I knew how cute Cynthia Lucinda
thought Edward G. was.
I'd have to trade a lot
to get him back.

When I got to Cynthia Lucinda's house,

Edward G. was busy doing

what he does best.

He was insisting on coloring

Cynthia Lucinda's pink wallpaper

with red and black crayons.

He was insisting on
wrapping himself up like a mummy
in her brand-new dress.

And he was insisting on
smashing bananas in her hair.
When Cynthia Lucinda saw me,
she crossed her arms.

She looked really mad.

"This wasn't a fair trade,
Evelyn J.," she said.

"You didn't tell me about
Edward G.'s insisting."

I showed Cynthia Lucinda
all the great stuff I brought
to trade for Edward G.

But in the end,

the only thing she wanted

was her Beautiful Pink Hairbow back.

When Edward G. and I got home,
Mom hugged him and gave him his dinner.
Then, because I hadn't read him
his before-dinner story,
Edward G. insisted on
an after-dinner story.

I guess it wasn't a bad
trading day after all.
Cynthia Lucinda hadn't had time
to find out one last thing
Edward G. insists on . . .

. . . cuddling warm against you
while he falls asleep in your lap.